Written by Tim Collins

Illustrations by John Bigwood

Front cover illustration by Joëlle Dreidemy

Thanks to Collette Collins, Philippa Wingate and Bryony Jones

First published in Great Britain in 2014 by Buster Books,
an imprint of Michael O'Mara Books Limited,
9 Lion Yard, Tremadoc Road, London SW4 7NQ

 www.busterbooks.co.uk

 Buster Children's Books

 @BusterBooks

www.cosmiccolin.co.uk

A CIP catalogue record for this book is available from the British Library.

ISBN: 978-1-78055-242-2

10 9 8 7 6 5 4 3 2

Printed and bound in March 2014 by CPI Group (UK) Ltd, 108 Beddington
Lane, Croydon, CR0 4YY, United Kingdom.

Papers used by Michael O'Mara Books are natural, recyclable products
made from wood grown in sustainable forests. The manufacturing processes
conform to the environmental regulations of the country of origin.

COSMIC COLIN

Sneezy
Alien Attack

BUSTER

CHAPTER ONE

This is a bin.

This is my friend Harry jumping into it.

And this is me, following him right in.

Why are we jumping into a bin?

Because it's not really a bin at all,
of course.

It's a spaceship that can take us

ANYWHERE
IN SPACE AND TIME.

Strange things happen every time we get
in it.

Like the time we were captured by aliens
with giant noses.

CHAPTER TWO

My little brother David is **REALLY** annoying.

This is me.

This is David.

He's not just annoying in the way that **ALL** brothers and sisters are.

He's **COMPLETELY** annoying.

He deliberately messes around in front of
the screen when I'm at a difficult bit in
a computer game.

David!
Get out of the way.

He turns the lights on and off all the time
and shouts, 'Disco!'

He says the word 'cool' all the time like it's the most hilarious thing ever.

And he **ALWAYS** has a cold.

Mum **NEVER** wants to know.

MUM! Tell David to stop sniffing!

It's not his fault. He's got a cold.

Yeah, but he's doing it really loudly on purpose.

You'll have to tell him yourself, Colin. I'm busy!

So I have to keep listening to his horrible sniffles.

Mum never thinks David does anything wrong.

One day, I tried to take my mind off things by playing my bowling computer game.

It was going really well. I'd scored eleven strikes in a row.

Just one more and I'd have bowled a PERFECT GAME for the FIRST TIME EVER.

I got my player into position, put just the right amount of spin on the ball, and ...

CHAPTER THREE

Harry couldn't have picked a better time to land the spacebin in our garden.

I thought about what
might happen ...

It's too risky.

Harry shrugged and wandered back to the spacebin. It looked like I was doomed to a day of listening to David snivelling.

But then Harry stopped.

I've just thought of something. I could take you to Epsilon B. It's a completely empty planet, so there's no way David will be able to annoy anyone.

CHAPTER FOUR

Epsilon B was **AWESOME**. It's the only planet in the galaxy with a non-stop log flume. It's like a normal log flume in a theme park, but it lasts forever, because it goes all the way round the planet.

Harry showed me on his space communicator.

Epsilon B: front

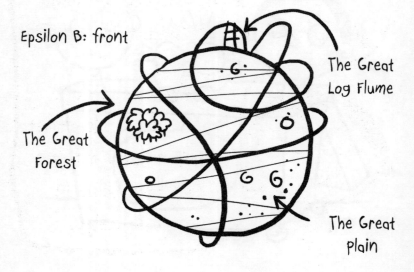

The Great
Log Flume

The Great
Forest

The Great
Plain

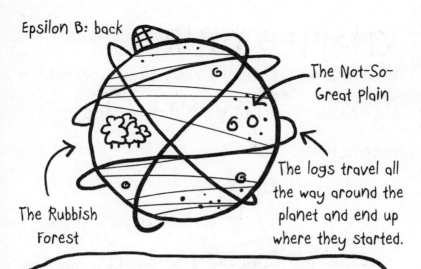

Epsilon B: back

The Not-So-Great plain

The logs travel all the way around the planet and end up where they started.

The Rubbish Forest

Okay. We all need to jump on to the logs, lie down and grab them tight. Some of the drops are very steep, so you need to cling on for the whole time.

When we've gone round the whole planet we'll all jump off and go back home in the spacebin.

These were very simple instructions.
Which is why I should have been worried.
My brother can NEVER follow simple
instructions.

Harry jumped
on to a log and
clung on tight.

I jumped on to
a log and clung
on tight.

David jumped on to a log behind me.

I don't know why I let him go last. I should have made him go in front so I could keep an eye on him.

WHEE!

I was enjoying the
log flume so much,
I forgot to check
on David.

WHEE!

I couldn't believe it when I did. Even on a planet with no one around, David still wanted to show off.

The drop went on for **AGES**. At the bottom, I plunged into the cold water, still clinging to my log with all my strength.

I bobbed back up again and saw Harry on his log floating next to me, spitting out a mouthful of water.

David's log popped up next. But David wasn't on it.

CHAPTER FIVE

We clambered on to the muddy shore of the river.

There was no reply.

It was SO TYPICAL of David. He'd disappeared, and now we had to walk to the top of a steep hill that was really hard to climb.

David!

We clambered up, calling his name until we were out of breath.

Nothing.

I was muddy and drenched in sweat by the time we got to the top.

There was still no sign of my brother.

He must have gone into that forest. Let's go and look for him.

Okay, just give me a minute to get my breath back.

There was a large pile of rocks at the top of the hill.

I leant
against one
for a moment.

GRRRRRRRRRRRRRRR!

Are you hungry?

The rocks lurched and started moving. They weren't rocks ...

... they were **MONSTERS!** There must have been over a hundred in total.

Quick, let's run to the forest. We might be able to lose them in there.

CHAPTER SIX

We ducked into the forest just as the first of the monsters was about to grab us.

As I pelted through the thick trees, I heard the heavy stomps of the monsters fading into the distance.

Stomp!

I collapsed to my knees. The whole ground was covered in bright, smelly flowers. Pongs of strawberry, mint, banana, liquorice and lemon wafted up my nose.

It was weird to have all those smells filling my nostrils at once. It reminded me of the afternoon Mum spent hours trying out perfumes in a shop, and David and I got so dizzy we had to lie down.

I'll just try one more.

I thought you said this planet was empty.

I could have sworn it was. I might have been getting it mixed up with Epsilon D, though.

GREAT! So what are those things?

They're called 'Chompers'. They're the most horrible monsters in the universe.

They land on planets, eat everything and everyone, and only leave wreckage behind. Look.

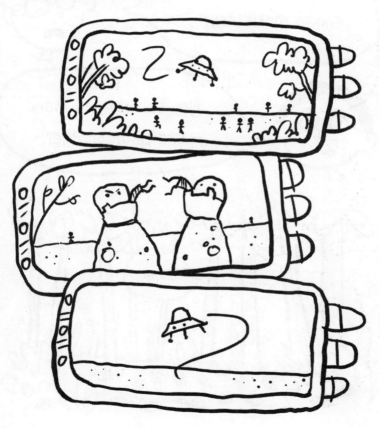

Colin, I think I just heard something.

Not another of those monsters?

No. It sounded more like your brother.

Choo!

We ran over to where the noise had come from. But when we got there, the noise had gone further away.

Every time we ran towards the noise, it moved.

Eventually we arrived in a clearing.

CHAPTER SEVEN

What are they? Do you think they're dangerous?

It's alright, leave it to me. I'm good at talking to aliens.

Harry leaned over to one of the creatures and spoke in a soft voice.

We mean you no harm. We're just looking for someone. Do you understand?

The creatures threw heavy sacks over our heads and tied them with string.

The creatures dragged us for ages over bumpy ground.

They didn't listen to Harry:

I'll give you ten thousand space dollars if you let me out.

Or to me:

I'll give you a PlayStation and five games if you let me out.

Things were no better when they finally let us out of the sacks.

Please set us free. We mean you no harm.

It's no use. They don't understand.

I grabbed the bars of my window and stared out at the darkening sky. We were in prison **AND** we'd lost David.

CHAPTER EIGHT

Harry spent all evening listening to the creatures and jotting things down on his space communicator.

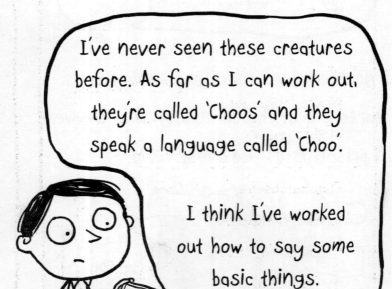

I've never seen these creatures before. As far as I can work out, they're called 'Choos' and they speak a language called 'Choo'.

I think I've worked out how to say some basic things.

Harry handed me his communicator.

HOW TO SPEAK CHOO

Hello	Choo!
Goodbye	Choo choo!
Please	Choo. Choo!
Thank you	Choo! Choo.
Please let us out of this prison.	Choo. Choo! Choo choo choo! Choo. Choo. Choo.
This has been a terrible mistake so if you could let us go free, that would be fabulous.	Choo.

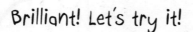

Brilliant! Let's try it!

We jumped up and down to get the Choos' attention.

Choo. Choo! Choo choo choo! Choo. Choo. Choo.

I said, 'Choo. Choo! Choo choo choo! Choo. Choo. Choo.'

A couple of minutes later, the Choos threw another sack into our cell.

Something stinky crawled out ...

... it was David. They'd found him!
Brilliant news!

YAY!

Cool!

Then I realized it wasn't brilliant news at all. I was still in prison, only now I'd have to put up with David's sneezing, too.

CHAPTER NINE

Achoo! Achoo!
Achoo! Achoo!

David's cold was even worse next morning.
Now he was even more annoying, if that
was possible.

Achoo!
Achoo!
ACHOO!
ACHOO!

Choo?

Choo?

The guards seem very interested in David.

They probably want to eat him. Do you think they'll set us free if we let them?

I've got it! They think David's speaking Choo. If we can find a way to control his sneezes, we could make them understand us. Try getting behind David and covering his mouth and nose. Then uncover them briefly when I nod at you.

Nooo! I'll get David's sneeze juice all over my hands.

This is important. It could get us released from here.

Alright then . . .

I stuck my hands over David's slimy nose and mouth and took them away when Harry nodded.

It was like playing the world's most disgusting recorder.

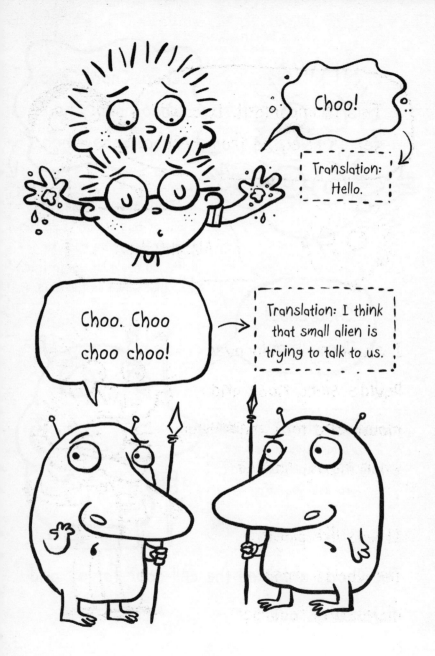

The Choos unlocked the cell door for us and marched us out.

CHAPTER TEN

It turned out we'd been in the basement of a huge palace. Hundreds of Choos stopped to stare as we walked past.

The creatures led us through endless corridors.

We walked past a bathing room, where rows of Choos were dipping their noses in large basins.

We walked past a bedroom where some Choos were sleeping on beds of paper tissues, snoring as loudly as jet engines.

Every room was stuffed with the bright flowers we'd seen in the forest. The sickly sweet whiff was so strong at times that I felt jealous of David for having a cold.

We ended up in a large room.

The Choo king was sitting on a lavish throne.

Harry translated as the Choos spoke.

Choo choo choo. Choo choo?

Translation: What are these hideous creatures with tiny noses?

Choo choo choo. Choo choo. Choo choo choo!

Translation: Some animals we found in the woods. They want to speak with you.

Harry nodded at me and I operated
David again.

Choo choo
choo choo.

Translation: Thank you
so much for agreeing to
see us, Your Majesty.

Choo. Choo?

Translation: Well I never.
These animals really do talk.
And what is it you want?

Harry nodded at me again. I tried to operate David, but he sneezed so hard my hands slipped, and I couldn't follow Harry's instructions.

ACHOO!

CHOO CHOO CHOO CHOO CHOO CHOO CHOO CHOO CHOO!

Translation: Let us go, you big-nosed freak!

The king looked very angry.

Oh dear, that came out wrong! Let's try again.

This time I kept my hands steady and carried out Harry's instructions correctly.

As Harry explained how we came to be in the forest, a large crowd of Choos gathered in the throne room to stare at us.

Choo. Choo.

Translation: They must be so ashamed of their freakishly small noses.

Choo, choo, choo.

Translation: These talking animals are so weird.

Choo! Choo! Choo!

Translation: I want one of those talking animals, Mummy! I demand that you buy me one!

When we got to the part in our story about the Chompers, the crowd's reaction turned to anger.

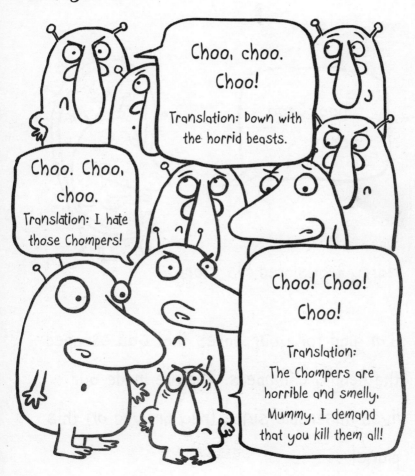

CHAPTER ELEVEN

The king sighed and shook his head when we'd finished.

Choo. Choo choo . . .

Harry translated his story.

'I'm glad for your sakes that you escaped the deadly Chompers. They've made our lives miserable since they arrived on this planet . . .

'We lived here peacefully for hundreds of years. We devoted our time to growing beautiful flowers that filled our nostrils with sweet smells.

'Then the Chompers came. Soon a whole army of them was eating everything in sight. It was the worst disaster since the great hayfever outbreak of 14007.

'Sometimes they ate things raw. At other times, they cooked them in foul-smelling sauces that offended our sensitive nostrils.

'And afterwards, they had terrible bouts
of wind that offended our sensitive nostrils
even more.

'My father led a group of Choos and went
to confront them. He told them to go
home and leave us in peace.

'The Chompers ate the Choos without even
bothering to answer. They probably didn't
understand what my father was saying,
but it was still very rude.

'We retreated into the forest, where Chompers never seem to venture.

'We're safe in here, but we'd do anything to get rid of the foul-smelling beasts and have the planet to ourselves again.

'We long to roam the hills and plains and ride the beautiful log flume without having to worry about getting eaten. But we probably never shall.'

CHAPTER TWELVE

When the Choo king had finished speaking,
Harry gave me some instructions to
operate David.

Choo. Choo!
Choo! Choo.

Translation: We'll help you
defeat the Chompers if you
promise to set us free. We,
er, just need a bit of time to
work out some of the details.

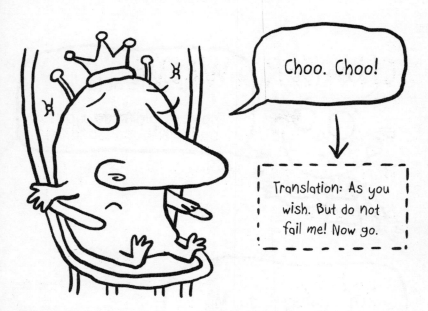

Choo. Choo!

Translation: As you wish. But do not fail me! Now go.

The Choos marched us back through the palace and locked us in our cell again.

You don't actually have a plan, do you?

Of course I do. My plan is to get YOU to come up with a plan.

I had just a couple of hours to work out a way to defeat the Chompers and win our freedom.

PLAN ONE: DESIGN A POSTER ABOUT PEACE AND WRITE A MOVING SPEECH CONVINCING THE CHOMPERS TO MAKE FRIENDS WITH THE CHOOS.

Hmm. The Chompers will probably eat the poster AND us.

PLAN TWO: CAPTURE THE CHOMPERS AND TRANSPORT THEM BACK TO THEIR OWN PLANET IN THE SPACEBIN.

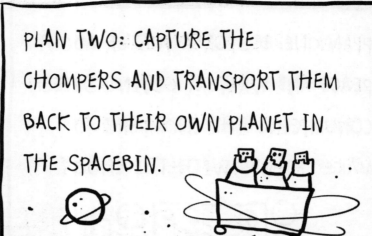

But we might end up taking the Chompers back in time or to the wrong planet by mistake. They could do something bad like eat the Romans.

PLAN THREE: POISON SOME FOOD AND LEAVE IT OUT FOR THE CHOMPERS. THEY'RE SO GREEDY THEY WON'T BE ABLE TO RESIST IT.

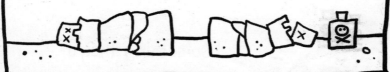

But what could poison the Chompers? They eat everything on every planet they go to, and it doesn't seem to harm them.

Everything I came up with seemed wrong.

But then I thought of something. Maybe there **WAS** something on the planet that could poison the Chompers ...

... something they'd avoided, even though they ate **EVERYTHING** else.

CHAPTER THIRTEEN

We went back to see the king and I operated David to describe the plan.

The king thought about it for a moment and nodded. A few minutes later, we set off for the edge of the forest again. Only this time, we were honoured guests rather than prisoners.

Then we prepared our attack. It was all very simple — I'd worked out the reason the Chompers wouldn't go in the forest. It was because of all the flowers!

The flowers must be poisonous to Chompers.

All we had to do was gather huge piles of flowers and lob them at the Chompers.

The Choos set up catapults on top of the hill. They blew their war bugles.

Chompers crowded on to the plain below.

We set off the catapults, pelting the
Chompers with flowers.

Then we pelted them again.

And again, using the last of our supplies.

The Chompers gobbled up the flowers and continued up the hill. They didn't look very poisoned.

All the Choos turned to look at me.

Well, this is awkward.

Er ... looks like the flowers aren't so deadly after all.

So why won't the Chompers go into the forest?

They're probably just too big to fit under the trees.

ROAR!

Ouch.

Oh. That could explain it too, I suppose.

The Chompers let out loud roars as they made their way up the hill.

CHAPTER FOURTEEN

The Choos fled back into the forest, leaving us to face the army of Chompers alone.

Those Choos are a bunch of cowards.

I know.

I heard something scrabbling behind me. I turned and saw David running up the hill.

Come back, David! This isn't the time for messing around.

David ran behind one of the big rocks.

Bowling, cool.

What? Why are you being so annoy—

Wait! I think he's on to something.

We ran up to David. He was trying to push
one of the rocks.

Quick! We need
to help him.

We leapt behind the rock and helped David
shove it. It shifted forward, slowly at first.
But it rolled faster and faster as it headed
for the first group of Chompers.

I couldn't believe it. David had actually come up with a good idea for once.

The boulder had wiped out the first group of Chompers. But there were still loads of them coming up the hill towards us.

And there are eleven groups of Chompers coming for us ...

That means ... to defeat them, we're going to have to bowl the perfect game.

We got behind the first boulder and started to play.

2ND STRIKE!!

3RD STRIKE!!!

4TH STRIKE!!!!

5TH STRIKE!!!!!

6TH STRIKE!!!!!!

7TH STRIKE!!!!!!!

8TH STRIKE!!!!!!!!!

9TH STRIKE!!!!!!!!!!

10TH STRIKE!!!!!!!!!!!

11TH STRIKE!!!!!!!!!!!!

12TH ... UH-OH!

The final boulder had missed the last group of Chompers completely. They rushed up the hill, gnashing and snarling ...

... closer and CLOSER.

GRRRRRRRRRRRRRRR.

Huge rocks hurtled down from the top
of the hill. By removing the boulders,
we'd started a massive landslide that was
heading right for us.

I ran towards the forest and leapt out of
the path of the stones.

I landed on the ground, just inches away
from the rumbling landslide. A huge cloud of
dust billowed over me, filling my eyes, ears
and nostrils.

Phew! Harry and David had avoided the stones, too.

When the dust cleared, I looked back down the hill. All the Chompers, including the ones who'd been chasing us, were completely buried now.

VICTORY!

CHAPTER FIFTEEN

It was only now that the cowardly Choos ventured back out of the forest. When they saw that all the Chompers were defeated, they jumped and snorted with joy.

They lifted us in the air and carried us home.

Choo! Choo! Choo! Choo! Choo! Choo!

Translation: Hail to the tiny-nosed heroes.

That night, the king threw a huge feast in our honour.

The Choos stuck their noses over their plates and inhaled all their food in a single snort.

I was amazed. Even David can't polish off a whole meal that fast.

I think the Choos were pretty confused when we started eating with our mouths instead of our noses, but they didn't say anything.

Maybe it's rude for them to talk with their noses full.

After the meal, the king took us to his throne room.

He proudly unveiled statues of us.

I **THINK** they were supposed to be flattering. So I said thanks.

Then it was time to leave. I'd have liked to have had another go on the log flume, but I didn't want to risk any more disasters.

The Choos showered us with pongy petals
as we clambered into the spacebin.

I was looking forward to getting away
from all those flowery smells. Even the
stink of David's room would come as a relief
after those.

Delicious!

CHAPTER SIXTEEN

Harry set the spacebin's controls to arrive back at my house a minute after we'd left.

We climbed out and David raced over to the house.

OH NO!
That's one of the Choos' flowers!

Quick, grab it! We must never bring anything back from space to Earth. If that flower touches the ground **ANYTHING** could happen. It might turn into a giant, man-eating plant.

The giant plants could spread across the world and turn the human race into slaves. It would be a disaster.

I ran over to David and grabbed the flower from his back.

Good! Now destroy it as quickly as possible.

I could only think of one way to make sure the alien flower would never touch the soil.

I put it in my mouth and ate it.

It was disgusting. It tasted of perfume
and sprouts. But I had to do it to save the
human race.

Harry took off again and we went inside and slumped on the sofa. Weirdly, I didn't find David's sneezes annoying anymore.

Sniff!
Achoo!
Cool!

After all, we'd never have been able to defeat the Chompers or befriend the Choos without him.

I never thought I'd say this, but I'm glad we took David along with ...

No. I take that back.

He's still **REALLY** annoying.